An Extraordinary Friend

Olivier Bonnewijn – Amandine Wanert

THE ADVENTURES OF JAMIE AND BELLA

An Extraordinary Friend

MAGNIFICAT® - Ignatius

Table of Contents

Chapter 1 Lost

A thin layer of frost covered the enormous train station of Lokavitch. The place was swarming with people. Jamie and Bella jumped up and down with excitement. The twins, their parents, their younger sister, Lily, and their little brother, Bubba, had been on the train all day. It was the first day of their holiday in a strange new country visiting relatives.

"We're on holiday!" sung Jamie, his jacket flapping open.

"Wow, it's slippery!" shouted Bella.

Jamie was getting ready to explore his new surroundings when his father's deep voice brought him up short.

"Jamie, will you please wait?" he commanded. Scooping up Bubba into his arms, he told Lily to take Mom's hand. "Mind you stick close to us, you two," he ordered the twins.

"Jamie, zip up your jacket," Mom added, "and give Bella your hand."

"Give Bella my hand?" grumbled Jamie to himself. "I'm ten and a half!"

"Jamie, do as you're told," scolded his mother. "You can easily get lost in these crowds."

Annoyed, Jamie took the end of the strap dangling from Bella's backpack. The Biltons pushed their way through the throng at a snail's pace. Jamie kept bumping into his sister.

All of a sudden, he was pushed by a particularly noisy group of tourists. In the confusion, he let go of the strap.

"They're rude!" thought Jamie to himself. "First they push into me and step on my toes, and then they don't even apologize." He was cross.

Looking up, he realized he could no longer see Bella's bag. And his mom and Lily weren't there either, or his dad with Bubba. There wasn't even a trace of the large green suitcase that his father had been wheeling along! Jamie scurried ahead, looking for them.

"Excuse me, excuse me, let me through, please!" Jamie said desperately, weaving his way through the crowds. But there was no sign of them anywhere. It was as if they had been swallowed up.

"Dad, Mom!" screamed Jamie, who by now was running frantically having lost all sense of direction. No one noticed him. No one listened. He had never felt so alone and abandoned. He couldn't even speak the language of all these strangers, and anyway they were only interested in catching their trains.

"Dong! Dong! Dong!" The station's clock struck ten. Jamie had been trying to find his family for almost an hour. He had searched down endless passages. He had climbed hundreds of stairs and peeked into a dozen empty rooms, but there was no sign of his family!

He had never felt so miserable. Exhausted, he sank into a corner and pulled the zipper of his

jacket up to his chin. He crossed his arms around his knees and put his head down and moaned: "Lord, help me! I want to see my dad and my mom. Please do something. I beg you."

Chapter 2 A Cardboard Shelter

Sudden shouting startled Jamie. Near him he saw three big bullies punching and kicking a boy who was lying on the ground. The boy was screaming in pain.

"Three against one, how unfair!" thought Jamie. "What brutes!" Without another thought, he ran towards the bullies, yelling at the top of his lungs to scare them. The boys fled at once.

"Are you in pain?" asked Jamie as he knelt by their victim. The boy uttered something and slowly got up. His nose was bloodied, and his clothes were torn and dirty.

"Do you want my jacket?" asked Jamie. The boy didn't respond.

Jamie took his jacket off and placed it awkwardly around the boy's shoulders. He remembered

seeing a waiting room. It wasn't far away, and he managed to steer his companion to it.

"Look, here's a radiator in the corner," he said. "You'll feel better in a minute. Oh, and by the way, what's your name?"

The child shrugged his shoulders unhappily. He didn't understand a word.

Jamie tried again: "Me, Jamie. I'm Jamie," he repeated slowly, pointing to himself. "And you?" he signed.

"Popov," answered the boy, at last understanding.

The children sat on the floor and lapsed into silence. Popov was worn out from the attack. His head gently slid onto Jamie's shoulder, and he fell asleep. Jamie soon dozed as well.

"вставай! ми закриття!"[1] called out the booming voice of the station guard, waking Jamie roughly. Jamie blinked, looked round him and realized that Popov was gone. His jacket was gone too. Jamie was left feeling more alone than ever and even a bit betrayed. He began to get really worried. Perhaps the guard would help him. He tried his best to explain himself, but the guard took no notice. He just shoved Jamie towards the door.

"біжи! ми закриття!"[2] he said in a gruff voice. Jamie found himself in a dimly lit hallway. A draft of cold air caught him. Tears ran down his cheeks, and he felt completely miserable. Just then, he heard someone calling his name: "Jamie!"

He looked round eagerly. It wasn't Mom or Dad. It was Popov, holding a thick grey blanket. Popov handed Jamie back his jacket and gave him a

1 Translation: "Get up! We're closing!"
2 Translation: "Run along! We're closing!"

curiously warming smile. He then beckoned, inviting Jamie to follow him. Jamie noticed that he was still limping badly.

Popov led Jamie to a secluded corner of the station. He showed him where they could find some cardboard boxes, and together they dragged along enough to build a makeshift shelter. Finally, Popov spread out his blanket, and they both lay down.

Chapter 3 A Morning Stroll

"Dong! Dong! Dong!" The great clock struck six. An early train was about to depart. Jamie opened his eyes and looked around him. "Where am I?" he thought as he gazed at the cardboard ceiling. Then he remembered the hardships of the previous day and cried out: "Mom! Dad!" He was relieved to see that Popov was still at his side.

"Гей Jamie. Як спалося?" [3] asked Popov.

"Hi!" answered Jamie, who didn't understand a word of what his friend had said.

"Хочете їсти? Хочете випити?"[4] asked Popov again.

Acting on his words, Popov handed Jamie three stale biscuits and a cup of cloudy water.

"Oh, thanks Popov! Thank you!" said Jamie, cheerfully.

"Yuck," thought Jamie to himself. "This looks awful. But I'm starved, and it might offend Popov if I refuse."

It didn't take long to finish breakfast. The boys then decided to stretch their cramped limbs to try to get warm. They walked toward a nearby square and scared away a group of pigeons. They were happy to be together. They even laughed for no reason.

3. Translation: "Hey Jamie! Did you sleep well?"
4. Translation: "Do you want to eat? Do you want to drink?"

As they were about to cross the street, Popov's nose started bleeding.

"Hold on," said Jamie, taking his friend's arm and resting him on the ground. He'd often had nose bleeds himself but never as bad as this one. Soon the hanky he'd pulled out could hold no more.

He was relieved when the blood stopped, but they needed to do something to clean up Popov's face.

"I know. There's a fountain over there," he said, nudging his friend toward it. "Put your head back, and I'll clean you up."

"Your feet are also bleeding now!" exclaimed Jamie, looking down from his labors. "Look at your socks! Let me take them off. No wonder you limp. You should have told me. Those ruffians really beat you up yesterday," he added with feeling.

Popov then pulled up his shirt. An old wound had reopened between his ribs. Bravely, Jamie cleaned out the cut with the fountain's very cold water. He ripped his own shirt into pieces to make bandages for Popov.

"There we are. It's all done. When I've found my parents, we'll take you to a real doctor," he said reassuringly.

Sitting back, Jamie noticed for the first time the large blue and white building that dominated the square. It resembled a palace. Its roof was covered with golden domes in the shape of onions. Jamie was curious, and with a questioning stare he pointed at it.

"What is it?" asked Jamie.

"Це церква"[5] answered Popov, making the sign of the cross and pretending to pray.

A "tserkva"[6] repeated Jamie, who had never seen anything like it. He wanted to go inside. He had always loved churches, ever since he was tiny. They made him feel at home.

"Can we go to the tserkva[7]?" he asked, waving in its direction.

Popov nodded and led the way.

5. Translation: a church
6. Translation: a church
7. Translation: a church

Chapter 4 Illumination

J amie paused inside the door of the imposing building. Hundreds of candles were flickering in the darkness. The smell of incense filled the air. His eyes were drawn to a large crucifix ornamented with gold and silver that hung above the main aisle. Popov knelt down reverently.

Folding his hands, Jamie began to pray as he had never prayed before. He recalled with a heavy heart how he had refused to take Bella's hand and all that had happened since. Images of the pushing crowds and of Bella's disappearing backpack flashed through his mind.

"Dear Lord, I beg you, help Daddy and Mommy to find me. Otherwise, what's going to happen to me?" he mumbled in a whisper.

"Thank goodness for Popov!" he thought. He remembered how Popov had slept on his shoulder. When he had been cold and homeless, Popov had

offered him his cardboard home. When he had been hungry, Popov had given him some stale biscuits to eat. When he had been thirsty, Popov had given him some water to drink.

Jamie smiled and turned toward his Savior on the cross. He contemplated the crucifix at length.

A soft glow emanated from Jamie's face as he prayed.

"And Popov," he puzzled to himself. "Who are you? Where do you come from? Who are your parents?"

"Your face, your feet and your side must be in such pain from the blows you received," he thought.

He was calmed by being in the presence of God. He looked now at Jesus with fresh eyes.

He was particularly drawn to the blood flowing from Christ's face and hands, as well as from his feet and his heart.

"You're just like Popov," Jamie realized slowly.

"The wounded head and hands, and the pierced side–Popov and Jesus are one and the same!" he whispered.

A strange but wonderful feeling came over him.

Then, out of nowhere, a familiar voice cried out: "Jamie!"

His heart leapt and he turned round. He couldn't believe his eyes. It was Bella, running toward him and shouting: "Dad, Mom, come quick! He's here!"

Never before had he been so happy to see his sister. Tears of joy and relief streamed down both twins' faces. Jamie's parents arrived a few seconds later, still visibly shaken but trembling with joy.

Lily and Bubba charged into their big brother.

"Oh, Jamie! You gave us such a terrible fright," cried his mother as she squeezed her elder son in her arms.

"We searched for you all night," said Jamie's dad. "We went to the police, to the embassy and even to the army. This morning we came to this church to beg God's mercy on us and to ask him to find you."

"You must be frozen," said Jamie's mom pulling his jacket close and zipping it up. "Here, you can have my hat and scarf."

"Jamie! Jamie!" yelped Lily and Bubba, who were jumping up and down.

"Tell us what happened to you!" Bella put in.

Jamie freed himself from the grabbing arms and looking round him said: "I must introduce you to Popov."

"Popov? Who's he?" asked Lily and Bella together.

"He looked after me when I was lost and left alone in the dark," Jamie answered, looking round. "He's my new friend. Popov!" he called.

"Who are you talking about?" asked Bella, following his gaze.

"He's there, just beneath the great cross. Come here, Popov," said Jamie walking up the aisle.

"But there's nobody there!" exclaimed Bella, shrugging her shoulders.

"Popov?" cried out Jamie. "Popov! Popov!" he repeated, running toward the altar.

But there was no answer. Popov had vanished.

Reading Key:
To Better Understand the Story

1. **Does Jamie react well when he loses his parents?**

No, he does not. Instead of staying put, he runs frantically in every direction. He should have patiently waited for his parents to return.

2. Is Jamie courageous?

Jamie faces many challenges in the story. He loses his parents and witnesses the violence of bullies. He also suffers from the complete indifference of the station guard. He endures the bitter cold night air and dresses Popov's wounds. Despite all this, Jamie shows great inner strength. He does not shy away from his troubles but confronts them bravely. He stands firm despite being tempted at times to give up. With energy, determination and intelligence, he overcomes the obstacles one after the other. Jamie demonstrates true courage. When he is reunited with his family, he is proud of himself and has reason to be.

3. Who is Popov?

What do you think? The story doesn't tell us where he is from or whether he has a family. Neither do we know what he does all day or where he gets his food. We first encounter him in a poorly lit hallway, beat up on the floor. At the end of the story, he disappears without explanation.

4. Is Popov "Jesus in disguise" ?

Yes, in a way. Popov saves Jamie not only from the darkness of the night and the cold but also from hunger, solitude and fear. Popov is accustomed to praying in churches. His wounds are like those of Jesus: on the head, the side and the feet.

There is a strong resemblance between Popov and Jesus. Jamie realizes this at the end of the story. Jamie senses the mystery that Christ is particularly present in the poor and weak: "I tell you the truth, whatever you did for one of the least of these brothers of mine, you did for me" (Matthew 25: 40). That is why theologians sometimes say that the poor are like a sacrament; they render Jesus present, alive and visible.

5. How can we help the poor?

At the start of the story, Jamie helps Popov who is poor and hurt. He defends Popov against the brutes, lends him his jacket, brings him to a warm waiting area and sits by him.

In the second part of the story, Popov is the one helping Jamie. He offers him a place to sleep, brings him something to drink and consoles him.

Look at the beautiful drawing on the cover of this book. It is just like Jesus with the Samaritan woman (John 4: 7). Who is giving and who is receiving in the image? Jamie not only gives of himself in the story, he also receives by letting Popov help him. Lost and alone, Jamie desperately needs Popov's help, reassurance and friendship. Popov now has the joy to serve, to love and to be loved. This is the best way to help the poor: to give and to receive.

6. Do Jamie and Popov become true friends?

During their morning walk to warm up, Jamie and Popov feel happy in one another's presence. They understand each other without speaking the same language. They help one another to do what's right, and they do not abandon their friend when he is in trouble. Jamie and Popov trust each other, and they know their friend can always be counted on. They have become true friends.

Do you think there is a difference between a true friend and a person who is only an acquaintance?

7. Why does Jamie enter the church?

Since his baptism, Jamie has always felt at home in church. There are thousands of churches on earth where God, our heavenly Father, dwells. Under the Virgin Mary's loving gaze, Jamie is reunited with his father, his mother, Bella, Lily and Bubba.

8. Why does Popov disappear at the end of the story?

This is a difficult question to answer. It is a mystery that escapes us. In fact, this is a true story even if certain details have been changed. And this is the way it ended. Perhaps you may have an idea...

Translated by Marthe-Marie Lebbe
Cover illustration by Amandine Wanert

Original French edition:
Les aventures de Jojo et Gaufrette : Un ami extraordinaire
© 2009 by Édition de l'Emmanuel, Paris
© 2012 by Ignatius Press, San Francisco • MAGNIFICAT USA LLC, New York
All rights reserved.
ISBN Ignatius Press 978-1-58617-772-0 • ISBN MAGNIFICAT 978-1-936260-46-1
The trademark MAGNIFICAT depicted in this publication is used under license
from and is the exclusive property of MAGNIFICAT Central Service Team, Inc.,
A Ministry to Catholic Women, and may not be used without its written consent.

Printed by Friesens on August 24, 2012
Job Number MGN 77141
Printed in Canada, in compliance with the Consumer Protection Safety Act of 2008.

The Author

Olivier Bonnewijn

Father Olivier Bonnewijn has been a priest of the Archdiocese of Brussels in Belgium since 1993 and is a member of the Emmanuel Community. He teaches at the Institute for Theological Studies in Brussels.

The Adventures of Jamie and Bella were conceived during summer catechetical camps. The children's thirst for truth and their contagious enthusiasm inspired the stories, which are all based on true accounts. Father Bonnewijn had the joy of witnessing many of them.

The Illustrator

Amandine Wanert

Amandine Wanert lives in Paris. She illustrates both for medical journals and for children's literature. Fascinated by the world of children, she spends time observing them in public parks and in school settings to fuel her imagination. Jamie's and Bella's physical features are in part based on her childhood memories. Bringing to life The Adventures of Jamie and Bella in harmony with Father Bonnewijn's text has been a joyful and enriching experience for Amandine.